Traci Sorell • Illustrated by Madelyn Goodnight

POWWOW DAY

i◠i Charlesbridge

For Liz, Cierra, and others who returned to the circle,
and in memory of those who could not—T. S.

To my wonderful family, who taught me what
unconditional love and support mean—M. G.

At the time of publication, all URLs printed in this book were
accurate and active. Charlesbridge, the author, and the illustrator are
not responsible for the content or accessibility of any website.

Published by Charlesbridge, 9 Galen Street, Watertown, MA 02472
(617) 926-0329 • www.charlesbridge.com

Printed in China
(hc) 10 9 8 7 6 5 4 3 2 1

Illustrations done in digital media
Display type set in Breakfast Burrito designed by © David Kerkhoff
Text type set in Colby designed by © Jason Vanderburgh
Color separations and printing by 1010 Printing International Limited
    in Huizhou, Guangdong, China
Production supervision by Mira Kennedy
Designed by Cathleen Schaad

Library of Congress Cataloging-in-Publication Data
Names: Sorell, Traci, author. | Goodnight, Madelyn, illustrator.
Title: Powwow day / Traci Sorell; illustrated by Madelyn Goodnight.
Description: Watertown, MA: Charlesbridge, [2022] | Includes
    bibliographical references. | Summary: Because she has been
    very ill and weak, River cannot join in the dancing at this year's
    tribal powwow, she can only watch from the sidelines as her
    sister and cousins dance the celebration—but as the drum
    beats she finds the faith to believe that she will recover and
    dance again.
Identifiers: LCCN 2018058514 (print) | LCCN 2018060774 (ebook) |
    ISBN 9781580899482 (reinforced for library use) |
    ISBN 9781632898159 (ebook)
Subjects: LCSH: Indian girls—Juvenile fiction. | Powwows—Juvenile
    fiction. | Indians of North America—Rites and ceremonies—
    Juvenile fiction. | Indian dance—Juvenile fiction. | CYAC:
    Powwows—Fiction. | Indians of North America—Rites and
    ceremonies—Fiction. | Dance—Fiction. | Sick—Fiction.
Classification: LCC PZ7.1.S6777 Po 2022 (print) | LCC PZ7.1.S6777
    (ebook) | DDC 813.6 [Fic]—dc23
LC record available at https://lccn.loc.gov/2018058514
LC ebook record available at https://lccn.loc.gov/2018060774

"River, wake up," Amber whispers.

My eyes open.

Today is powwow day!

Then I remember.

No dancing.

No jingle dress competition for me.

Not at this tribal powwow.

"I wish my hair weren't still so short." I sigh.

Mama lays out the moccasins that match my dress.

"But everyone wants to see *you*," Amber reminds me.

"Why? I can't dance like I could before I got sick."

"But you *will* dance again," she responds.

I stay silent
as Daddy drives us
to the powwow grounds.
I usually savor
the scents of sage
and sweetgrass,
but not today.
The breeze prickles
my skin.
I'm tired already.

Daddy arranges our chairs
near the family drum.
Mama squeezes me close. "Doing OK?"
I nod, but I'm not.
I watch my friend Dawn get ready to dance.

No, I'm not OK.

Then the powwow begins
as the emcee calls,
"Time for Grand Entry—stand up.
Gentlemen, remove your hats."
My uncles strike
a large drum together.

BAM. BAM. BAM. BAM.

They sing,

**"EH-yah,
EH-yah,
WEY-eh-yah-ah."**

I make a decision.
"At least I can dance Grand Entry."
"You *sure*?" Amber asks.
"Yup."

Grandpa leads with the eagle staff.
Other warriors carry flags into the arena.

BAH-dum.
   BAH-dum.
      BAH-dum.
         BAH-dum.

Elders head up the long line.
Oldest to youngest—
traditional,
fancy,
grass,
and jingle dress.

Dawn squeezes my hand as
we wait with Amber
and the other girls
to dance into the arena.
My feet stay still.

I can't feel the drum's heartbeat.

Amber grabs my arm.

"You OK?"

She leads me back to our seats.

Everyone dances in
and moves around the circle,
all connected to
the drum,
Mother Earth,
and one another.
Everyone.
Amber, Dawn,
our cousins,
our friends.
Everyone but me.
I watch
through wet eyes.

After Grand Entry, an elder prays that
our dances honor the Creator,
that our culture and language will stay strong,
and that healing will come
to those who need it.

Like me.

I rise to join
the intertribal dance.
But I can't focus.
Mama's steady hand
guides me into my seat.

The drum's heartbeat
surrounds me.

BAM.

BAM.

BAM.

BAM.

I lean against Daddy
and watch the competitions.
Traditional dancers move
and draw me in
to their story.
Fancy dancers twirl
and ribbons whirl.

Graceful grass dancers sway
and weave themselves
around the circle.
The drum starts its beat inside me.

Then the emcee calls . . .
"Girls' jingle dress—
head to the arena."
For a second
my heart leaps.

But I can't do
the healing dance today,
even though I need it.
Dawn said she'll dance for me.

My heart swells as
I see Dawn, my sis,
our cousins,
and friends
step and turn,
graceful and fast.
Their feather fans wave.
Rows of cones *clink*
clink
clink
on their dresses.

I sit up tall as they come close.
Judges move around
the powwow arena
and record scores . . .
but the girls don't dance
for the judges.

They dance for
the Creator,
the ancestors,
their families,
and everyone's health . . .
including mine.

BAH-dum.
BAH-dum.
BAH-dum.
BAH-dum.

I stand.
I open my heart.
I feel the drum fully now.
Then I know . . .

I will join them at
the next powwow.

I *will* dance again.

Information About Powwows

Powwow: Powwows are celebrations of dance, song, culture, and community, mostly originating from the warrior societies of the Ponca and Omaha tribes on the northern and southern plains of North America. Native Nations, universities, and nonprofits across the United States and Canada host powwows year-round. They last from one to four days and are held outdoors as well as inside large gymnasiums or meeting spaces. Some powwows feature competitions like the one in this story, where dancers compete for cash prizes. Others are traditional. Some are held to honor a specific person, celebrate special events like graduations, or provide a service, such as free health screenings for attendees. Everyone is welcome at a powwow and is expected to follow the event etiquette.

Arena: The designated area for dancing at a powwow, blessed prior to the event, is called an arena. It includes

the emcee's table, drum groups, and seating for dancers and their families. Spectators sit beyond this area. Once an arena is blessed, it is a sacred place during the event. One can only enter it to dance: no walking, running, or cutting across to the other side is allowed. No disruptive behavior, alcohol or drug use, or bad language is permitted within it. Outside the dance arena, vendors sell food, jewelry, artwork, and clothing.

Emcee: The emcee is the host who guides the dancers, drum groups, and spectators to keep the powwow program moving. This person announces the upcoming dances or competitions, explains powwow traditions, and tells stories—often funny ones—to entertain the crowd. The emcee explains powwow etiquette for spectators, including how touching a dancer's regalia (traditional outfit and accessories) is not allowed, and when and where photography or recording devices are allowed.

Arena Director: This person organizes the dancers for Grand Entry, selects judges for contest dances, and maintains order in the dance arena or circle during the powwow.

Grand Entry: This occurs when all dancers process into the arena by age and style of dance regalia (traditional outfit and accessories). The audience is expected to stand, and men are expected to remove their hats. The host drum group sings the Grand Entry song, followed by other drum groups offering honor songs (such as flag songs and veterans' or victory songs). Two esteemed dancers called the Head Man and Head Woman lead the procession. Veterans and active-duty military enter and present the flags. The eagle staff enters first, followed by flags from Native Nations as well as the state, national, and often the POW/MIA (Prisoners of War / Missing in Action) flags. Then tribal dignitaries— elders and other special guests—dance in after the flags. The rest of the dancers in their regalia follow, lined up oldest to youngest by dance style—traditional, fancy, grass, and jingle dress.

Host Drums and Drum Groups: These are groups of men who offer the dance music by sitting around a large drum, beating it with long sticks and singing a variety of traditional songs and vocables (song words that have no translated meaning, such as eh-yah or fa-la-la). The powwow activity revolves around their music. There is at least one drum at every powwow, but usually there are several. The emcee announces which drum group will perform each song at the powwow.

Dances: The dances at a powwow rely on the drumbeat, which dictates the beginning and end of the song and the pacing that dancers must follow. Intertribals are non-contest dances in which everyone can participate. They are led by the Head Man and Head Woman. Male traditional dancers' movements tell stories about traditional hunts or battles, while women represent their family and tribe through dignified steps. Fancy dances display a man's or woman's physical stamina to perform complex steps to the drum's quick beat. Grass dancers focus on maintaining balance as each side of the body mimics the other through intricate footwork and swaying torso.

Jingle Dress Dance: Rows of tiny cone-shaped metal jingles or bells dangle from the dancer's dress and strike against one another as she moves. One of the dancer's feet must always remain in contact with the earth while dancing. The dance is often considered a prayer for healing. Dancers may privately receive gifts of tobacco from others at the powwow and be asked to pray for an ill family member when they dance at the public event.

The jingle dress dance originated in an Anishinabe/Ojibwe healing ceremony in the Great Lakes region of North America toward the end of World War I while a flu epidemic raged worldwide. Maggie White, a

young Ojibwe girl of the Naotkamegwanning First Nation, became seriously ill. Her father sought a vision of how she might be cured. In his vision, he received instructions about how to make a dress and how to have Maggie wear it and perform dance steps. Upon doing the dance, Maggie recovered. From there, the Jingle Dress Dance Society grew and later came to involve dancing beyond the Ojibwe bands, and eventually led to the present-day practice at powwows nationwide.

During the COVID-19 pandemic, jingle dress dancers across Canada and the United States shared videos online of themselves dancing in their homes or outside for all people affected by the terrible disease.

Author's Note

I attended my first powwow in college and learned to cook big, fluffy frybread to sell for the Native student group fundraiser. Neither powwows nor frybread are traditional to my tribe, the Cherokee Nation. But I love the community that powwows foster among tribes and how non-Native people are invited to attend to learn more about contemporary Indigenous cultures.

Sources:

"American Indian Powwows: Multiplicity and Authenticity—History." Smithsonian Center for Folklife and Cultural Heritage, accessed April 12, 2018, https://folklife.si.edu/online-exhibitions/american-indian-powwows/history/smithsonian.

Browner, Tara. *Heartbeat of the People: Music and Dance of the Northern Powwow*. Urbana: University of Illinois Press, 2002.

"History of Powwows." Canadian Encyclopedia, accessed April 13, 2018, http://www.thecanadianencyclopedia.ca/en/article/history-of-powwows.

Horse Capture, George P. *Powwow*. Cody, WY: Buffalo Bill Historical Center, 1989.

Joseph, Nancy. "A Pow Wow Primer." University of Washington College of Arts and Sciences, 2006, accessed April 14, 2018, https://artsci.washington.edu/news/2006-07/pow-wow-primer.

"Powwow Dances." Canadian Encyclopedia, accessed April 15, 2018, http://www.thecanadianencyclopedia.ca/en/article/powwow-dances.

"Powwow: Native American Celebration." Encyclopedia Britannica, accessed April 14, 2018, https://www.britannica.com/topic/powwow.

"Powwow Regalia: Rites and Protocol." City University of New York, accessed April 13, 2018, http://digital-archives.ccny.cuny.edu/exhibits/What_Not_to_Wear/WNTW_7_Powwow.pdf.

Zotigh, Dennis W. "Powwows." Oklahoma Historical Society, 2006, accessed April 15, 2018, http://www.okhistory.org/publications/enc/entry.php?entry=PO030.